Dragons don't read books

D0993001

Other books in the Shooting Star series:

Dragons don't read books

Brenda Bellingham

illustrations by Carol Wakefield

Scholastic Canada Ltd.

Canadian Cataloguing in Publication Data

Bellingham, Brenda
  Dragons don't read books

(Shooting Star)
ISBN 0-590-74081-4

I. Wakefield, Carol. II. Title. III. Series.

PS8553.E468D73 1992   jC813'.54   C92-094238-5
PZ7.B45Dr 1992

Copyright © 1992 Brenda Bellingham. All rights reserved. No part of
this publication may be reproduced or stored in a retrieval system, or
transmitted in any form or by any means, electronic, mechanical,
photocopying, recording, or otherwise, without written permission of
the publisher, Scholastic Canada Ltd., 123 Newkirk Road, Richmond
Hill, Ontario, Canada L4C 3G5.

7 6 5 4 3 2 1   Printed in Canada   2 3 4 5 6/9
                 Manufactured by Webcom Limited

Contents

Chapter 1

It's a Bookworm

"My name's Jeff Brown," Jeff said, when anybody asked him.

Jeff's parents had named him Justinian Edwin Frederick Fotheringham Brown. "To make him different from all the other Browns," they said.

But Jeff didn't want to be different. He was medium-sized with brown hair and brown eyes. Ordinary looking. He used his initials and called himself Jeff. "I'm Jeff Brown," he said. "Just an ordinary guy."

And so he was — until he met the dragon.

* * *

On Tuesday it was the fourth grade's turn to have library period. Right away they saw something new lying on top of a bookcase.

"Isn't it fun?" asked Mrs. Page. "It's going to be our library mascot." She beamed at everybody. As well as being the school librarian, Mrs. Page was the grade four teacher.

The mascot was about three metres long. Its rear end came to a point. Yellow squiggles ran around its green body. It had red, glittering eyes and a sharp snout. The inside of its grinning mouth was as red as fire. Jeff wondered what it was supposed to be. He thought it wouldn't be polite to ask.

Bruno didn't care about being polite. He was a big, strong kid with blond hair and red cheeks. Bruno lived next door to Jeff. He and Jeff always walked to school together, and home again afterward.

"What is it?" Bruno asked.

Mrs. Page glanced over at the story corner. The kindergarten class was there, sitting quietly around on cushions. Their teacher was reading them a story.

"I had to tell the little ones what it was," Mrs. Page said, "but I thought you grade fours could figure it out for yourselves. Bruno, what do you think it is?"

Bruno scowled to help himself think. He tipped his head to one side to get a better look. "A sausage," he said at last.

Poppy Rose screamed with laughter. "A green sausage!" she cried.

"With mustard." Sally giggled, pointing at the yellow squiggles.

"And a mouthful of ketchup," added Poppy Rose.

Bruno didn't like to be laughed at. He glared at Poppy Rose. "You need new glasses," he said.

"These are new," said Poppy Rose. "They're the latest style."

Mrs. Page turned to Jeff. "Jeff, what do you think our mascot is?"

Jeff wished she hadn't asked him. He didn't like to look stupid in front of the other kids. He didn't like to look smart either. He didn't like to stand out at all.

He studied the thing on the bookcase. It was a gigantic stuffed toy, the kind he'd always wanted to win at the fairground, but it wasn't fuzzy. It was smooth and shiny, like silk. He hesitated.

"Well," he said, "It looks kind of like a worm."

"That's right, Jeff," said Mrs. Page. "It *is* a worm."

"A worm!" said Bruno scornfully. "I never saw a green and yellow worm before."

"Where did you get it, Mrs. Page?" Sally asked.

"From Mr. Bronski, the school janitor," answered Mrs. Page. "He won it at the fair, but he doesn't have room for it in his apartment. I thought it should live in our library."

"Why?" asked Bruno.

"I know," said Poppy Rose. "It's a bookworm. Right, Mrs. Page?"

Mrs. Page smiled. "Right, Poppy Rose."

Tilly Perkins put her hand in her skirt pocket.

She pulled out a pair of glasses and set them on her nose. She peered at the worm.

"Wrong," said Tilly Perkins.

Jeff smiled. Tilly Perkins wasn't ordinary. For one thing, she didn't wear ordinary clothes, like jeans. "I'm going to be a princess when I grow up," Tilly had once said. "Princesses don't wear jeans."

Tilly Perkins stood with her skinny legs apart. As usual, her tights were wrinkled like two corkscrews. Her blouse had lost a button. Tilly wore a dandelion through the leftover button hole. Another one was stuck behind her left ear.

"I beg your pardon, Tilly," Mrs. Page said.

Tilly glared at the bookworm. Her new glasses had blue plastic frames. Little bits of gold swam inside the plastic like goldfish swimming in a blue pond. The frames swept up at the corners like wings. Tiny diamonds glittered on the wings. Tilly's glasses weren't the latest fashion, like Poppy Rose's. They were prettier, thought Jeff.

He tried to nudge Tilly. She hadn't heard the

warning in Mrs. Page's voice. If she had, she didn't pay any attention. Tilly didn't notice Jeff's nudge. If she did, she didn't understand.

"It's not a bookworm," said Tilly. "It's a dragon."

"A dragon!" squealed Poppy Rose. "You sure are dumb, Tilly Perkins. Dragons have spikes down their backs, don't they, Mrs. Page?"

"And they breathe fire," added Sally. She pretended to look scared.

"And they have wings so they can fly around and grab people," said Bruno. "Then they take them back to their caves to eat. Only there's no such thing as a dragon."

"This is a baby dragon," said Tilly. "It hasn't grown its wings yet. It doesn't breathe fire right now, but if you ever make it mad, look out."

"Tilly," said Mrs. Page, "dragons are fierce. Our bookworm isn't fierce. Can't you see its big grin?"

"That's not a grin," said Tilly. She squinted at the worm through her new glasses. "It's a snarl. A sneery snarl."

"That will do, Tilly," said Mrs. Page. "Everybody, choose your books. When we go back to our room, we're going to write letters. I want you to thank Mr. Bronski for giving us our friendly bookworm." She went to help the class find any special books they wanted.

"I hate writing letters," Bruno muttered, clenching his teeth. "It's all your fault, Tilly Perkins. You and your dragon. You made Mrs. Page mad. I'd like to feed you to a dragon, only there's no such thing. Maybe I'll just beat you up."

Did Tilly Perkins quake?

Did Tilly Perkins quiver?

No, she did not. Tilly Perkins shrugged. "I like writing letters," she said. "I'm going to ask Mr. Bronski to take the dragon away before it causes trouble."

"Don't be stupid, Tilly Perkins," said Poppy Rose. She looked down her nose through her nifty new glasses. "It's a worm. Anybody can see that."

Tilly Perkins smiled knowingly. "Worm is

another name for dragon," she said.

Sally looked at Tilly Perkins and smirked. "Prove it," she said.

"Okay," said Tilly. "Wait while I find *The Dragon Hunter's Handbook*."

Chapter 2

Magic Glasses

Tilly Perkins isn't ordinary, thought Jeff. Still, she isn't stupid either. He went to help her find *The Dragon Hunter's Handbook.*

They searched the shelf. The book wasn't there. They looked on the nearby shelves. All they found was two kindergarten kids hiding behind a bookcase. Jeff knew them. So did Tilly. Everybody in the school knew Bertha and Ferdinand.

Bertha and Ferdinand were always getting into trouble. On the way to school they stopped to play and were late. Sometimes they went home at recess. Once they rolled a ball down the hallway and nearly knocked the principal down like a bowling pin. They giggled in Assembly. Bertha and Ferdinand weren't afraid of anybody — not even the principal.

Jeff and Tilly looked down over the top of the bookcase.

"What are you doing?" Jeff asked.

"Hiding," said Bertha.

She and Ferdinand gazed up at Jeff and Tilly, wide-eyed. Bertha's eyes were blue. Ferdinand's were brown.

"You should be in the story corner," said Jeff.

"We don't want to," said Ferdinand. "We've read that story twenty times. It's boring."

"Read another book," said Jeff. "We've got lots in the library."

"We've read all the ones we like," said Bertha.

"What kind do you like?" asked Tilly.

"Books about dragons and princesses," said Bertha. "Look at me. I can stand on my head." She turned herself upside down. Her skirt fell over her head.

Jeff blushed. "Bertha, stand up. It's rude to show your underwear," he said.

Bertha ignored him.

"This library needs some new books," said Ferdinand. "We've read all the good ones."

"That's not true," said Jeff. "You're only in kindergarten."

Tilly put her head close to Jeff's. The dandelion behind her ear tickled his nose. Her new glasses bumped against his cheek. "I think it *is* true, Jeff," she whispered. "Bertha and Ferdinand could read before they started school."

Ferdinand began to wiggle across the floor on his stomach. Mrs. Page came along with her arms full of books. She tripped over Ferdinand. The books went flying.

"Ferdinand, what are you doing down there?" she asked crossly.

"I'm a bookworm," said Ferdinand. "Can I be the library mascot?"

"No," said Mrs. Page, nodding at the book worm. "We already have one. Would someone

pick up these books for me please? Bring them to my desk."

Bertha's legs came down with a crash. Her face was bright red from standing on her head. She pointed at Tilly Perkins. "*You* said it was a dragon," said Bertha.

"It *is* a dragon," Tilly said firmly. "Watch out."

"A dragon!" Bertha gave a wobbly smile.

"A dragon!" Ferdinand blinked hard.

Jeff had never seen them look scared before. They must believe in dragons, he thought. He turned to Tilly. "Now look what you've done," he said. "You've scared two little kids."

Did Tilly Perkins admit she'd been foolish?

Did Tilly Perkins agree she'd fibbed?

No, she did not. Tilly Perkins frowned. "Stay away from that dragon," she said. "Dragons are dangerous." Then she picked the books up off the floor and took them to Mrs. Page.

"Is it true?" Bertha asked Jeff. "Is it really a dragon?"

"Of course not," Jeff said. "Tilly Perkins likes

to pretend. It's a bookworm."

"What do bookworms eat?" asked Bertha.

Jeff thought for a minute. "I guess they eat books," he said.

"That's what I thought," said Bertha.

Ferdinand began to wiggle across the floor again. "I'm a bookworm," he said. "Bookworms devour books."

"Devour?" Jeff said.

Tilly's head popped up over the bookcase. "It means the same as eat," she said.

"I know that," said Jeff, but he really hadn't been sure. "If he means eat, why can't he say so?"

"Ferdinand likes big words," said Tilly. "He and Bertha are very smart."

Bertha was standing on her head again. Ferdinand was wriggling across the floor.

"They sure don't act smart," said Jeff.

"And they have very good imaginations," said Tilly.

"I think they're a pain," said Jeff. "Let's try to track down that dragon book you wanted."

Tilly put her arm around Jeff's shoulders. Luckily no one was looking. "You're smart, too, Jeff," she said.

"I don't want to be smart," said Jeff. "I like being the way I am. Ordinary."

Tilly Perkins stared at Jeff. "Jeff, you're not ordinary," she said. "You're extraordinary. Just you wait and see."

It wasn't true, thought Jeff, but it was nice of Tilly to say so. He looked through the book cards. "Maybe someone borrowed the dragon book," he said.

"You're wasting your time, Jeff," said Tilly. "Dragons don't sign out books. They're too lazy."

"Tilly," said Jeff, "we're too old to believe in dragons."

Tilly looked shocked. She peered at Jeff through her magic glasses.

"Jeff," said Tilly Perkins, "nobody's ever too old to believe in dragons."

Chapter 3

A Clue

Nobody had signed out *The Dragon Hunter's Handbook*.

"Bet there's no such book," said Bruno.

"Tilly Perkins tells lies," said Poppy.

"Tilly Perkins, why are you wearing those freaky glasses?" asked Sally. "I bet they're not even real."

Did Tilly Perkins flush?

Did Tilly Perkins fume?

No, she did not. Tilly Perkins smiled. "My glasses are special," she said. "They help me see."

"That's what glasses are for," said Poppy. "What's so special about that?"

"My glasses help me see what's true," said Tilly Perkins. "They're magic."

"Magic glasses!" squealed Poppy.

"Tilly Perkins believes in magic," shrieked Sally.

"Be quiet," said Mrs. Page. "Libraries are for people who want to read."

As soon as they got back to their room, the class had to write their thank-you letters. Mrs. Page read them.

"Bruno," she said, "you must do your letter again. 'Thank you for the dum worm I still think it looks like a sossage,' is not polite. *And* it has two spelling mistakes and a missing period."

Bruno groaned.

Mrs. Page read Tilly's letter. "Dear Mr. Bronski," it said. "I'm sorry to tell you that the worm you gave Mrs. Page is really a dragon. It is not a friendly dragon. It is mean. At home I have dragons of my own, and so I can tell a mean one when I see it. Please take your dragon back to where you got it. It is not safe to be at school. Sorry to tell you such bad news. With deep sympathy, Tilly Perkins."

Mrs. Page raised her eyebrows. "Tilly Perkins, I'm surprised at you. I didn't think you'd be unkind to Mr. Bronski."

"I was only trying to help," said Tilly.

"It isn't helpful," said Mrs. Page. "It's very silly." She tore up Tilly's letter and dropped the pieces in the garbage can. "Mr. Bronski is new to our country. We should try to make him feel welcome."

"I'm sorry, Mrs. Page," Tilly said. "I'll write another letter to Mr. Bronski." She sighed. "People say I don't tell the truth. But I do. The trouble is, they won't believe the truth I tell."

"Tilly, I'm afraid you let your imagination run away with you," said Mrs. Page. "Now, I don't want to hear another word about dragons."

Tilly leaned over and whispered loudly. "Jeff, have you ever fought a dragon? If not, I think you'd better read up on it."

A few days later Mrs. Page stood at the front

of the room. She held a list. "These library books are missing," she said. "If anybody has one, please bring it back tomorrow."

She read out six titles.

"Mrs. Page," said Tilly, "all the missing books are from section 398."

"That's right, Tilly," Mrs. Page said. "But how does that help us?"

"I think it's a clue," said Tilly. "They're all fairy stories or folk tales. I think it has something to do with that dragon in our library."

Most of the kids laughed. Tilly was making up another story. Jeff didn't laugh. He wished it were true. A dragon in the library would be more fun than a bookworm, thought Jeff.

"Tilly Perkins is crazy," Poppy Rose said. She breathed on her glasses and cleaned them on a piece of soft cloth.

"Tilly Perkins thinks a stuffed toy can steal books," said Sally. She grinned.

"Tilly Perkins believes in dragons," said Bruno. "There's no such thing."

Maybe Tilly shouldn't pretend so much,

thought Jeff. The other kids think she's weird.

The next day the principal made an announcement. "I don't like to think that anybody in this school would borrow books and not bring them back," he said.

"What did I tell you, Jeff?" said Tilly. "More books from section 398 are missing."

"What does that prove?" Jeff asked.

"There are dragons in those books," Tilly said. "There's *The Dragon Hunter's Handbook* and *Dragon Folklore* and *A Book of Dragons*. And a lot of fairy tales tell about dragons. Dragons are vain. They like to read about themselves."

"Tilly," Jeff said. "dragons don't read books. Anyway, it's not a dragon. It's a stuffed toy. Have you ever seen it move?"

"You sure don't know much about dragons, Jeff," Tilly said. "They sleep in the daytime. Sometimes they sleep for years."

"With their eyes wide open?" Jeff asked, scornfully.

"Sure," said Tilly. "That's what makes them so hard to deal with. You never can tell if they're awake or asleep."

"I give up," said Jeff.

"The books might have been put back in the wrong places," said Mrs. Page. She asked Jeff and Tilly to search the shelves. Jeff glanced at the stuffed worm. It grinned widely.

"I think the bookworm looks friendly," he said.

"Dragons are good at fooling people," Tilly replied. "They're not honest."

Maybe she was right, thought Jeff. Crocodiles looked as if they were grinning, too. And crocodiles looked something like dragons . . . *Nah!* Tilly Perkins was making him imagine things. She was good at that.

"Forget the dragon," he said. "You're not looking very hard. Take off those stupid glasses so you can see properly. We promised Mrs. Page we'd try to find those books."

"Don't worry, I'll find the books. My magic glasses will help me," said Tilly.

Tilly Perkins always has to have the last word, thought Jeff.

Chapter 4

All Suspects

The next day, more books were missing. The principal asked all the classes to check their rooms.

"This is just like spring cleaning time at our house," said Poppy Rose.

She and Sally enjoyed cleaning out their desks. Bruno didn't. He scrabbled through his stuff. Pieces of paper fell on the floor. Bruno threw them in the garbage can. Then he sat down to watch the other kids.

"You didn't clean out your desk," said Sally.

"It's a mess," said Poppy Rose.

"I don't care," Bruno said. "I don't have any dumb library books."

"We'll clean out your desk for you," said Poppy Rose.

"We've finished ours," Sally said.

Bruno's desk was full of crumpled-up worksheets, old pieces of chewing gum, some leftover lunch, two odd socks and three mittens. There was even an old runner.

"Yucky," cried Poppy Rose, pulling a face.

"Stinky," said Sally, holding her nose. She held it out by the tip of one lace, at arm's length.

"Gimme that," said Bruno, grabbing it from Sally. "I wondered where that went."

There were no library books in Bruno's desk.

Poppy Rose and Sally peered over Tilly's shoulder and snooped in her desk.

Tilly lifted out her model of an African village. She was doing a report on Africa. Tilly had made a dragon out of Plasticine for her village.

"There aren't any dragons in Africa," Jeff said.

"Yes, there are," said Tilly. "There's a story

about a dragon in the book of African folk tales in our library."

"Prove it," demanded Poppy Rose.

But the book of folk tales from Africa had gone. No one had signed it out. It had simply disappeared.

"How come the books you read always go missing?" asked Poppy Rose.

"Looks fishy to me," said Sally.

There were no library books in Tilly's desk. Jeff had known there wouldn't be. Tilly Perkins wasn't ordinary, but she wasn't a thief either.

Later Jeff saw Mr. Bronski, the janitor, in the hallway. Usually Mr. Bronski smiled and talked to the people who went by. Today he leaned on his mop and looked sad.

"Mr. Bronski, what's wrong?" Jeff asked.

Mr. Bronski sighed. "When first I came to this fair land, I thought I would live happily ever after," he said.

Mr. Bronski was new to Canada. His English was new, too. It sounded good to Jeff, but different — as if Mr. Bronski had stepped out of a book. He was a very smart man. In his own country he'd been a philosopher. Mr. Bronski said that was someone who thinks a lot. There weren't many philosopher jobs in Canada. That was why he'd taken a job as a janitor.

"Aren't you happy anymore?" asked Jeff.

Mr. Bronski shook his head. "Alas, my happiness has fled. The principal thinks I am a thief."

"Why?" Jeff asked indignantly.

"Once upon a time, in the land of my birth, I knew a wise old woman," said Mr. Bronski. "Before I set forth on my adventures, I went to ask her blessing."

"And she told you to steal books?" Jeff asked, puzzled.

"Far from it," said Mr. Bronski. "She was wise, not wicked. 'Jacob Bronski,' she said, 'listen to me. You must learn the language of your new country. The best way is to read. Start with stories for little children and work your way up.' "

"And did you?" asked Jeff.

"Yes," said Mr. Bronski. "I followed her

advice to the letter. Every day, when my work is done, I read in the school library. Also, I borrow books to take home."

"But that doesn't mean you steal them," cried Jeff. "The principal should know that."

"I cannot find it in my heart to blame him," said Mr. Bronski. "Of late I have been reading fairy tales. *English Fairy Tales, Celtic Fairy Tales, The Blue Fairy Book, The Red Fairy Book, The Green Fairy Book.* All have vanished. It is as if an evil magician waved his magic wand. Poof! The books disappear."

It was true. Section 398 was almost empty. It looked bad. But Mr. Bronski wasn't a thief.

I'll go tell that stupid principal he's wrong, thought Jeff. It would take a lot of courage. His knees felt wobbly. Maybe if he put it off until tomorrow . . . I guess I'm not very brave, he decided. I'm just too ordinary.

* * *

"From now on, no one will be allowed in the library unless I am here," said Mrs. Page the next day.

"I don't see why I can't come to the library," said Poppy Rose. "I don't steal books."

"Neither do I," said Sally.

"I'm sorry, Poppy Rose and Sally," said Mrs. Page. "Everyone is a suspect. It's too bad. I wish the thief would own up."

Bruno looked at Jeff. "You and Tilly Perkins could have taken them. You're monitors. You get to be in the library after school."

"I don't think Jeff would steal," said Poppy Rose. "But Tilly Perkins likes books a lot."

"Especially books about dragons," said Sally. "She's always making up stories about dragons."

"Sally, that's no proof," Mrs. Page said. "It could be anybody."

"Even you, Mrs. Page," Bruno said. "You get to be in the library when no one else is here."

Mrs. Page's cheeks turned pink. "That's right, Bruno. We're all suspects."

But no one really suspects Mrs. Page, Jeff thought.

"Mrs. Page," said Tilly, "why is the dragon

lying on the floor?" She peered at the book worm through her magic glasses. "If you ask me, that dragon's up to no good."

"Tilly, do you mean the bookworm?" asked Mrs. Page. Mrs. Page knew what Tilly meant. She didn't wait for an answer. "I put it on the floor for the kindergarten children to play with," she said.

"But they'll mess it up," said Poppy Rose.

"Now, Poppy Rose," said Mrs. Page. "The little ones love that bookworm. Bertha and Ferdinand were climbing the shelves to reach it. I was afraid they'd fall and hurt themselves."

"Mrs. Page, please don't let the little kids play with that dragon," said Tilly. "Especially Bertha and Ferdinand. Dragons are evil. They're a bad influence."

"Tilly Perkins, take off those glasses," said Mrs. Page. "You'll ruin your eyes. And how many times do I have to tell you? Our mascot is not a dragon. It's a bookworm. Now that the little ones have gone, we can put it back on the shelf."

The worm was so long it needed a person at each end to lift it. Bruno and Jeff swung it up.

"Boy," said Bruno, "this dumb worm's heavier than it looks."

"Dragons can get to be real monsters," said Tilly.

But nobody paid any attention. They were tired of hearing about dragons.

School was no longer a happy place. Mr. Bronski didn't smile and say hi anymore. He kept his eyes on his mop.

"The principal thinks Mr. Bronski stole the books," Jeff told Tilly.

"Bruno and Poppy Rose and Sally think I did it," said Tilly.

Did Tilly Perkins look sad?

Did Tilly Perkins look sombre?

No, she did not. Tilly Perkins's brown eyes twinkled behind her glasses.

"Tilly, this isn't funny," Jeff said. He liked Tilly Perkins. He was her friend. He cared what people thought of her, even if she didn't.

Chapter 5

Tilly's Plan

At recess Ferdinand ran to Jeff. Bertha followed with her skipping rope.

"Is Tilly Perkins *really* a princess?" asked Bertha.

"Of course not," said Jeff. "She just likes to pretend."

"She won't let us in the library," said Ferdinand. "She says it's been closed by Royal Decree, whoever that is."

"Forget Royal Decrees," said Jeff. "It's closed by Mrs. Page."

"But we have to feed our bookworm," said

Bertha. "He's getting hungry." She tripped over her skipping rope.

Jeff smiled. "What does he like to eat?" he asked.

"Alphabet cereal for breakfast," said Ferdinand.

"Alphabet soup for lunch," said Bertha. She made it into a chant to skip to.

"What about supper?" asked Jeff.

"Anything," said Bertha. "He's not fussy."

"He has a voracious appetite," said Ferdinand. "Tilly Perkins says that proves he's a dragon. She says all dragons are greedy."

"But he's not really a dragon, is he?" asked Bertha. Her eyes were wide.

"No," said Jeff. "He's a bookworm. I've told you before. Tilly Perkins has a very good imagination."

Bertha skipped away. Ferdinand ran to play on the swings.

Poppy Rose, Sally and Bruno came up.

"How come Tilly Perkins gets to stay in at recess?" asked Poppy Rose.

"She's helping Mrs. Page put up some stuff in the library," said Jeff.

"I figured she was up to something," said Bruno.

"She's probably casing the joint," said Sally.

"Look," said Jeff. "Tilly Perkins is different, all right. But she doesn't steal books. And neither does Mr. Bronski."

"Who said anything about Mr. Bronski?" asked Poppy Rose.

"He wouldn't steal books," said Sally.

"He might," said Bruno. "He talks funny."

"He comes from someplace else," said Sally.

"So maybe he doesn't know you're not supposed to steal books," said Poppy Rose.

"He might be a spy," said Bruno.

"Spies don't steal library books," said Jeff. "And Mr. Bronski's nice. He doesn't put up notices telling you to take your boots off."

"I guess he's okay," Bruno admitted. "He doesn't get mad if you spill something."

"He helps you find your lost mitts and things," said Sally.

"We've got to find out who really stole the books," said Jeff. "Otherwise Mr. Bronski might get fired."

"And we don't want another janitor," said Poppy Rose.

"We might get a mean one," said Sally. "Like the one we had before."

"The kind that sends you to the office," said Bruno.

"What are we going to do?" Jeff asked.

"Catch the real thief, of course," said Sally.

"Sally and I will catch the criminal," said Poppy Rose. "We're partners. Detectives. Super sleuths."

"We'll get on the case right away," said Sally.

At that moment, Tilly Perkins bounded out of school with a hop, skip and a jump. Poppy Rose and Sally looked at Tilly, then at each other. They walked away, arm in arm, whispering behind their hands.

"Detectives! Those two couldn't even catch a cold," said Bruno. "Leave it to me. I'll tail the chief suspect. I'll get the truth out of that thief."

He gave Tilly Perkins a hard look and strolled away.

A minute later, Jeff saw Bruno's round red face peeping at Tilly from around the corner. This is awful, Jeff thought. The other kids really believe Tilly could be the book thief.

"Listen, Tilly," he said. "The principal suspects Mr. Bronski of stealing library books."

"The principal doesn't know about the dragon," said Tilly. "Mr. Bronski's kind. He makes the whole school feel friendly."

"Right," said Jeff. "So what can we do to help him?"

"We'll stay after school," said Tilly. "We'll hide in the library and catch the thief in the act. I already know who it is."

"Who?"

"The dragon," said Tilly.

"Not that dragon again!" Jeff said. "Tilly, I'm talking about the *real* thief."

"So am I," said Tilly.

"Forget it," said Jeff. "Anyway, we can't go to the library after school."

"Who says?" asked Tilly.

"Mrs. Page says," answered Jeff.

Did Tilly Perkins sigh?

Did Tilly Perkins surrender?

No, she did not. Tilly Perkins sniffed loudly. "Mrs. Page doesn't own the library," she said. "We'll ask Mr. Bronski to let us stay."

"Mr. Bronski doesn't own the library either," said Jeff.

"No, but he has keys," said Tilly. "He needs them so he can clean up."

"Tilly, are you serious?" Jeff asked.

He was afraid she was, and that meant trouble. Something was bound to go wrong. Jeff's stomach felt as if he'd been riding a fast elevator that had come to a sudden stop.

"I can't stay after school," he said. "My mom and dad know I don't help in the library anymore. I have to go straight home."

"I don't," Tilly Perkins said. "My mom will let me stay."

"Wanna bet?" Jeff said. He wished Tilly would smarten up or they'd never find the real crook!

Chapter 6

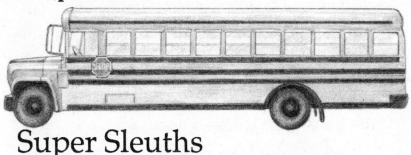

Super Sleuths

The next day, Tilly Perkins leaned over Jeff's desk. "It's okay," she whispered. "My mom says I can stay after school."

"I don't care what your mother says," said Jeff. "I can't stay."

"You can sleep over at my place," Tilly said.

Tilly Perkins can really make you mad, thought Jeff. She won't take no for an answer.

"I'll ask my mom to phone your mom," Tilly said. "Then on Friday you can come home on the school bus with me."

"We can't catch the book thief at your place," said Jeff.

"We'll miss the bus — by accident, on purpose," Tilly said. "Then I'll phone my mom to pick us up. I'll tell her to take a long time."

That won't be hard, thought Jeff. Tilly Perkins's mom always takes a long time. First she has to round up some stray farm animals, or her truck breaks down, or something else happens.

"It won't work," said Jeff. "One of the teachers will stay behind until your mom shows up."

"We can hide out in Mr. Bronski's room," said Tilly. "The teachers won't know we're still at school."

"What if someone finds us?" Jeff said. "Then they'll think for sure that you're the book thief. Me too. And if Mr. Bronski helps us, he'll be in trouble!"

Did Tilly Perkins wilt?

Did Tilly Perkins waver?

No, she did not. Tilly pulled her shawl around her shoulders, jammed her bonnet down over her ears, and set her glasses firmly on her nose. "No one's going to find us," she said.

Suddenly, Jeff noticed Bruno. He had sneaked up on them.

"How long have you been here?" he asked Bruno.

"Long enough," said Bruno. He looked pleased with himself. "I heard everything."

"Too bad," Jeff said. "We're not going to do it."

Bruno made clucking noises and flapped his elbows. "Tilly Perkins has a good idea for once in her life. I'll help her catch the book thief. *I'm* not a chicken."

Bruno was tough, no doubt about it. He wasn't scared of thieves. And he never cared if he got into trouble.

"I thought you said Tilly Perkins was the thief," Jeff said. "You sure changed your mind in a hurry."

"I only said I thought she was," said Bruno. "Anyway, if another thief doesn't show up, we'll know for sure it's Tilly."

Did Tilly Perkins fuss?

Did Tilly Perkins fret?

No, she did not. Tilly Perkins looked pleased.

"Tilly Perkins, you must be out of your mind," said Jeff. "Okay, you and Bruno go ahead with your dumb plan. See if I care."

He stomped away. On his way to the classroom he saw Mr. Bronski.

Mr. Bronski held out his hand to shake Jeff's. "I bid you a fond farewell," he said sadly. "I am banished from these beloved halls. I go to seek my fortune far from here."

"Have you been fired?" cried Jeff.

"No," said Mr. Bronski. "I have resigned."

"Why?" asked Jeff.

Mr. Bronski sighed. "After the robber removed all our fairy stories, I began reading myths. I borrowed *Beowulf*. I brought it back, but now that terrific tale is missing. Yesterday, I found the principal in my room. He was hunting high and low."

"Did the principal say what he was doing?" asked Jeff.

"Oh no," said Mr. Bronski. "He made many excuses. But I can read him like a book. I decided to depart. After I am gone the reading robber might strike again. That will prove my innocence."

"Wait," Jeff said. "When do you have to leave?"

"This coming Friday I will clean these halls of learning for the last time," said Mr. Bronski. Tears stood in his eyes.

Jeff made up his mind. Tilly's plan might be dumb. Tilly's plan might be dangerous. Still, it was the only plan they had. "Meet me in the janitor's room after school today," he whispered. "Tilly Perkins has a plan. We're going to catch the real thief. Then you won't have to leave."

Mr. Bronski wiped his eyes. "May the gods smile upon you," he said. He pushed his broad-headed mop away up the hallway.

"All right, Jeff Brown," said Poppy Rose's voice from behind Jeff. "What are you and Mr. Bronski cooking up? Sally and I saw you whispering together. Planning your next book heist, eh?"

"Who's your fence?" asked Sally.

"What are you two talking about?" asked Jeff.

"A heist is a robbery," said Sally. "And a fence is the person who sells your stolen loot."

"I know what a heist is," said Jeff. "And I know what a fence is. Mr. Bronski and I weren't talking about a robbery. He'd never steal anything. You two should be locked up."

Tilly and Bruno walked into school together. When they saw Poppy and Sally talking to Jeff, they stopped to listen.

"Jeff Brown, tell us what you were saying to Mr. Bronski," said Poppy Rose. "Or we're going to the principal. We'll tell him that you and Mr. Bronski are the book thieves."

"Poppy and I are super sleuths," said Sally. "You and Mr. Bronski are our chief suspects."

"I thought Tilly Perkins was your chief suspect," Jeff said.

"Her too," said Poppy Rose.

"She's probably in on it," said Sally.

Jeff groaned. "First Tilly Perkins thinks there's a dragon in the library," he said. "Now you two think you're the Hardy Boys."

"Guess it's up to you and me, eh, Jeff?" said Bruno. "On Friday I'll bring a rope to school. When the thief comes into the library, I'll wrestle him to the ground. Then you can help me tie him up. Okay?"

"Why Friday?" asked Poppy Rose.

"Because that's when we're going to stay after school. Right, Jeff?" boasted Bruno. "We're going to hide in the library. When the thief sneaks in, I'll bash him over the head. Then Jeff can help me tie him up."

"We want to help too," said Poppy Rose.

"It's only right," said Sally. "We're the detectives around here."

Tilly Perkins would never let Poppy Rose and Sally sleep over at her place, thought Jeff. They were always mean to her.

But Tilly nodded.

"Okay," she said. "You can both stay over at our place on Friday, too. My mom won't mind."

Jeff almost fell over with surprise. Tilly Perkins is a very forgiving girl, thought Jeff. She never holds a grudge.

She sure needs someone to look after her.

Chapter 7

They'll Ruin Everything

"What time is your mom going to pick us up tomorrow?" asked Bruno at lunch. "She might come before we catch the thief."

"She won't," said Tilly. "We'll phone her when we're ready."

"What if the thief doesn't come till late?" asked Jeff. "We can't stay here all night."

"Yes, we can," said Bruno.

"I'll bring some cookies in case we get hungry," said Poppy Rose.

"And I'll bring some juice boxes," said Sally.

"This isn't a picnic," said Jeff.

"Don't worry, Jeff," said Tilly. "It won't take long. As soon as it's dark the dragon will come out of its lair."

"Listen, you guys," Jeff said. "We're not playing games. Get serious, or I'm not helping on Friday."

"Jeff's got cold feet," said Bruno, grinning.

Poppy Rose and Sally grinned too.

Tilly looked admiringly at Jeff. Today she wore a necklace of dandelions strung together. The dandelions didn't smell very good. Tilly didn't seem to notice.

"Jeff isn't scared," she said. "He's the bravest boy in the world."

Jeff's cheeks got hot. He knew he wasn't the bravest boy in the world. He wasn't brave at all. He wished Tilly wouldn't say things like that.

The principal's voice came over the intercom. "Bertha and Ferdinand are missing again," he said. "Does anyone know where they are?"

Bruno pointed. One of the locker doors was not quite shut. With a sudden move, Bruno flung it open.

"Ta daa!" yelled Bertha, leaping out. "Here's Bertha."

"Surprise, surprise!" yelled Ferdinand, tumbling out after her. "Here comes Ferdinand."

Jeff and the others were too angry to say anything. They clenched their fists and glared at Bertha and Ferdinand.

Bertha and Ferdinand could see they were in trouble.

"Look at me," cried Bertha. "I can do cartwheels." She did a couple of clumsy cartwheels down the hallway.

"Watch this," cried Ferdinand. "I can leap like a frog." He crouched low and leaped after her.

Bruno pounced. With one hand he grabbed Bertha. With the other he grabbed Ferdinand. "Oh, no you don't," he said. "You're not getting away that fast."

"Let me go," said Bertha, wriggling.

"Me too," said Ferdinand, squirming.

"No way," said Bruno, holding them at arm's length.

"So much for Tilly's plan," said Jeff. "They'll blab it all over."

"How much did you hear?" asked Bruno, giving them a good shake.

"Nothing," squealed Bertha.

"Only an occasional word," squeaked Ferdinand.

Through her glasses, Tilly fixed Bertha and Ferdinand with a hard stare.

"Are you sure?" she asked. "You didn't hear us plan to stay after school on Friday? You didn't hear us say we'd hide in the library? You didn't hear that we're going to catch the evil dragon?"

Bertha's eyes opened wide. Ferdinand's mouth dropped open.

The others turned on Tilly.

"Tilly Perkins, are you totally crazy?" asked Poppy Rose.

"She simply has no smarts," said Sally.

Did Tilly Perkins look silly?

Did Tilly Perkins look sorry?

Yes, she did. "Oops," she said. "I guess I gave the game away."

Tilly Perkins was not crazy. Tilly Perkins was not stupid. Tilly Perkins *meant* to tell Bertha and Ferdinand, thought Jeff. She wanted them to believe in her dragon, but he didn't know why.

"Who cares if Tilly Perkins opened her big mouth," said Bruno. "These two had better stay away from that library. And keep their mouths shut. Or they'll be dead meat." He gave Bertha and Ferdinand an extra-hard shake and let them go.

"You catch our drift?" asked Sally.

Bertha nodded like a puppet with a loose head.

"Yes, ma'am," said Ferdinand. "We get the message."

Together, they ran away down the hall and sped around the corner.

"They won't bother us anymore," said Bruno. "They're too scared of me."

Jeff wasn't so sure. He thought he heard them giggling around the corner. Who knew what they'd do? Tilly's plan was getting riskier by the minute. How did I ever get into this, thought Jeff.

Chapter 8

Spoilsport

Jeff went to talk to Mr. Bronski after school. Bruno went with him. Poppy Rose and Sally saw Jeff and Bruno.

"Where are you sneaking off to?" asked Poppy Rose.

"We're coming too," said Sally.

This is no good, thought Jeff. They'll all try to talk at once. He was right. Finally, Mr. Bronski put up his hand.

"Please," he said. "Let Jeff speak for all."

When Jeff was finished, Mr. Bronski looked worried.

"Jeff, this is a splendid scheme," Mr. Bronski said. "But I fear for you and your friends. Those robbers might be murdering monsters."

"I don't think there's a gang of thieves, Mr. Bronski," said Jeff. "Just one."

"I don't care how many there are," boasted Bruno. "I can handle them."

"So can we," said Poppy Rose.

"Super sleuths are tough," said Sally.

"We don't have to *catch* anyone," Jeff said. "We just need to *see* the thief. Then we can tell the police who it is. Everything will be okay."

"Jeff, you speak like a true hero," said Mr. Bronski.

Jeff blushed. "I'm not a hero, Mr. Bronski. This was all Tilly Perkins's idea."

"Tilly Perkins thought of this plan?" Mr. Bronski asked. "The girl who draws dragons? The girl who paints pictures of craggy castles and dingy dungeons?"

Jeff nodded. "That's Tilly," he admitted.

"I have long admired Tilly Perkins's art," said Mr. Bronski. "She is wonderfully wise."

"She is?" asked Jeff.

"Tilly Perkins isn't wise," said Poppy Rose, lifting her nose in the air.

"She's a bird brain," said Sally, tossing her head.

"My heart is heavy," said Mr. Bronski. And he looked truly sorry. "Tilly's plan is clever and courageous. But I cannot lead you into certain danger. I must lock the library when I leave."

"You mean, you won't help?" asked Bruno.

"I cannot," replied Mr. Bronski.

"I told you Tilly Perkins's idea wouldn't work," said Poppy. She and Sally turned on their heels and stalked off.

"My dad's taking me to a football game, anyway," said Bruno. "Maybe the next janitor we get won't be such a spoilsport." He followed the girls out the door.

Jeff looked at Mr. Bronski.

Mr. Bronski smiled, but his smile was sad. "Your friendship has warmed my heart, Jeff. Let us see what fate has in store."

Outside, Jeff told Tilly what had happened.

Did Tilly Perkins look dejected?

Did Tilly Perkins look disappointed?

No, she did not. Tilly Perkins looked determined. "Don't worry, Jeff," she said. "I'll talk to Mr. Bronski."

Chapter 9

Terrible Tidings

Jeff and Tilly crept back to the janitor's room.

"I'm sorry to tell you this, Mr. Bronski," said Tilly Perkins. "I hope you won't feel too sad about it. But the worm you gave us isn't really a worm. It's a dragon."

"A dragon?" asked Mr. Bronski. He frowned at Tilly. "Are you sure, Tilly Perkins?" he asked.

"I'm sure," she said. "I know the signs. Day by day it grows larger. Hour by hour it looks fiercer."

Mr. Bronski sat down, *plop!* on an upturned pail. "These are terrible tidings," he said.

Now she's done it, thought Jeff. She's upset Mr. Bronski. He won't help us now. She's blown our last chance to catch the thief.

"As you know, dragons can't be trusted," said Tilly. "I have reason to think ours is mixed up in the book thefts."

"Don't listen to Tilly, Mr. Bronski," Jeff said. "She's always making things up."

Mr. Bronski sat on his pail, thinking. "I fear that Tilly could be right," he said at last. "Worm is another name for dragon. We would do well to listen to Tilly Perkins."

"We would?" asked Jeff.

"So you will help us, won't you, Mr. Bronski?" asked Tilly.

Mr. Bronski looked worried. "Tilly Perkins, dragons are dangerous."

Mr. Bronski should know better, thought Jeff. He shouldn't encourage Tilly and her dragon stories. He should worry about the real thief.

"The dragon won't hurt us," Tilly said. "Jeff will see to that. He's our knight in shining armour. He'll fight the dragon."

"Me? A knight?" Jeff was so shocked he almost fell over. "Me, fight a dragon? Tilly Perkins, you must be out of your mind."

Tilly looked thoughtful. "In the olden days princesses never fought dragons," she said. "That is true. Knights did it for them. But times have changed." She held her back straight. "I shall fight the dragon myself."

"Have it your way," Jeff said.

"Tilly," said Mr. Bronski gravely, "to fight a dragon you need a shining shield." He handed Tilly the lid from a metal garbage can. It was new and shiny. "The metal will reflect the dragon fire."

"And a lance," said Tilly.

Mr. Bronski handed Tilly a piece of his vacuum cleaner wand. "This will serve as your lethal lance," he said.

"A garbage can lid?" said Jeff. "Some shield! A vacuum cleaner wand? It isn't even sharp. That's not a real lance."

"Who can say what is real and what is not," said Mr. Bronski. "If you believe, a wand can

work wonders. And, Tilly, remember. A dragon's weak spot is its soft belly."

"Right," said Tilly. "That is where I will jab my lance."

"You'd better not," said Jeff. "What if you rip it? Mrs. Page will be mad."

"If I can't get at its belly," said Tilly, "I shall thrust my lance into the dragon's gaping jaws."

"You'll be sorry," said Jeff. "You'll tear that worm to shreds."

"I'd be sorry to slay the dragon," said Tilly. "After all, it *is* still young. But it's a chance I have to take."

Oh no, thought Jeff. She's totally flipped her lid!

"And now," said Tilly, "I'll go home and rest. I must keep up my strength. Not even a princess can fight a dragon without a good night's sleep."

When Tilly had gone, Jeff turned to Mr. Bronski. "If Tilly rips the bookworm she'll be in terrible trouble. People will think for sure she's a thief. And a vandal. She'll be expelled. We've got to stop her."

"Blame Tilly for slaying the dragon?" said Mr. Bronski. "You puzzle me."

"Mr. Bronski, you don't really believe in dragons," Jeff said.

"Indeed I do," said Mr. Bronski. "As we travel through life, many a dragon lies in wait."

Jeff lost his temper.

"Mr. Bronski, don't give Tilly Perkins the vacuum wand. She'll slash the worm. She'll slit it and slice it. She'll totally wreck that worm. Promise. Cross your heart and hope to die."

"But how will she fight the dragon?" asked Mr. Bronski.

"Stop talking about dragons," Jeff shouted. "I don't want to hear another word about dragons. I've had it with dragons. Dragons are dumb. Besides, *there's no such thing as a dragon.*"

Mr. Bronski looked sad. "Jeff, since you are so sure," he said. "I promise."

Chapter 10

Waiting for the Thief

At last Friday came. Bruno was on clean-up detail. At the end of the day he took the garbage to Mr. Bronski's room. Then he waited.

Poppy Rose was the blackboard monitor. She took the brushes outside to bash the chalk out of them. She took a long time. Then she dodged into the janitor's room.

Sally hung around the lockers. She said she was waiting for Poppy Rose. No one was surprised. Sally always waited for Poppy Rose. When nobody was looking, she crept into the janitor's room.

Who needs all this cloak and dagger stuff? thought Jeff. After school he walked to the janitor's room. If anyone asked, he could say he was going to talk to Mr. Bronski. That was true.

There was no sign of Bertha and Ferdinand. The kindergarten class had gone on a field trip to the fire station. Two extra parents had gone along to help — one each for Bertha and Ferdinand.

Thank goodness, thought Jeff. At least he wouldn't have to worry about them turning up. They were a pesky pair, but he didn't want them to get hurt.

Finally, Tilly arrived. "Everybody's gone," said Bruno. "Let's go hide in the library."

Tilly shook her head. "We can't just walk in there," she said. "The dragon will see us."

Bruno hooted. "Dragon!" he cried. "You're such a dummy, Tilly Perkins."

Poppy dug Sally in the ribs. "Dragon!" Poppy Rose said, giggling.

"Isn't she wild!" said Sally. She giggled too.

Did Tilly Perkins blush?

Did Tilly Perkins blubber?

No, she did not. Tilly Perkins looked sorry for Bruno, Poppy Rose and Sally.

I wonder if Tilly really believes in that dragon, thought Jeff. Or if she's only pretending. It sure is hard to tell.

"Who cares what Tilly Perkins says?" said Bruno. "I'll hide behind the library door. When the thief comes in I'll hit him over the head."

"No, you won't," cried Poppy Rose. "Sally and I will."

"It's only fair," said Sally. "We're the super sleuths."

"Hold on, Bruno," said Jeff. "What if Mrs. Page comes back to the library to do some work. You might hit her over the head by mistake. I've got an idea. The library doesn't have any windows."

"So what!" said Bruno.

"So the thief can't get away, except through the doors," said Jeff. "After the thief goes in, you wait outside. You hide near one door. Poppy

Rose and Sally hide near the other. Then you can nab him as he comes out."

"Good idea," said Poppy Rose. "The super sleuths will arrest the thief."

"With the hot goods on him," said Sally.

"Huh!" said Bruno. "Fat chance. He'll beat you up."

"Who said the thief's a him?" asked Poppy Rose.

"Right," agreed Sally. "Maybe she's a her."

"It's a him," said Bruno. "And, anyway, he'll come out of my door."

"You can *all* arrest the thief," Jeff said. "The doors aren't far apart."

"Right," said Poppy Rose. "Come on, Sally. Let's find a good place to hide."

"Well, okay," said Bruno. "But what about Tilly Perkins? What's she going to do?"

"Jeff and I are going to sneak into the library when the dragon isn't looking," said Tilly.

"Go right ahead," said Bruno. "Just make sure you don't make a noise when the thief comes. We don't want you messing things up."

"Tilly won't mess things up," said Jeff. "She's just fooling."

They waited until everything grew quiet. Mr. Bronski came in, pulling his vacuum cleaner.

"The coast is clear," he said. "Tiptoe to your places."

With a few smothered snorts and giggles, Poppy, Sally and Bruno crept away.

"Tonight I will clean as I have never cleaned before," Mr. Bronski said.

Tilly looked anxious. "Don't clean too hard, Mr. Bronski," she said. "The dragon might suspect something. Dragons are very smart."

Mr. Bronski nodded. "You are right. They are canny creatures. Sly and slinky."

"And they can see in the dark," said Tilly. "Remember that, Jeff."

The worm faced one door of the library. Tilly and Jeff crept in the other. The vacuum cleaner was very noisy. No one could hear them above that noise. Not even a dragon.

Jeff crept after Tilly. Why do I listen to Tilly Perkins, he wondered. I don't believe in dragons. All the same, his skin came up in goosebumps. Tilly Perkins is more fun than ordinary people, thought Jeff. She can make you imagine almost anything.

Tilly and Jeff each chose a bookcase to hide behind. Mr. Bronski finished cleaning. He put his vacuum cleaner out in the hall. He left the garbage can in the library.

It doesn't matter, thought Jeff. A shield isn't much use without a sword.

Mr. Bronski turned off the lights. As he left he banged the doors shut behind him. Outside, he fumbled with the locks. He made it sound as if he had locked the doors.

"To fool the dragon," Tilly had said.

So the real thief can get in, thought Jeff. He crouched behind his bookcase. He couldn't read because it was so dark. Tilly had a flashlight, but they couldn't use it.

"The dragon would see the light," Tilly had said. The real thief might see it, thought Jeff.

They couldn't talk, either.

"Dragons have sharp ears," Tilly had said.

The real thief might hear us, thought Jeff. Only Tilly and Mr. Bronski believed in dragons. But a real thief was just as scary.

Now that Mr. Bronski had gone, the library was full of black silence. You could hear the slightest sound. Jeff and Tilly waited . . . and waited . . . and waited. The floor began to feel very hard.

After a while Jeff stopped feeling scared. This is boring, he thought. Nothing's going to happen. The thief won't come. He probably heard about our plan.

Then he heard a noise. It sounded like someone chewing, and not very politely. *Smack, smack* went the person's mouth.

Tilly Perkins is eating her snack, thought Jeff. How can she feel hungry at a time like this?

He heard a hiccup. Then another. Tilly Perkins *would* have to get the hiccups, thought Jeff. If the thief comes, he'll hear her.

A dull thump came from somewhere. Jeff stopped feeling bored. Maybe Tilly bumped against her bookcase, he thought. Or else the thief's come. He felt shivery again.

Next he heard a scratchy sound, like someone putting something in the garbage can. What was Tilly doing? Why couldn't she keep still? He peeped around the bookcase. He couldn't see a thing.

A crash made him jump. It sounded as though someone had dropped a box of books. That wasn't Tilly. It must be the thief! His heart pounded.

Silently, he crawled out from his hiding place. The library looked like a black hole. Where was Tilly with her flashlight? He wriggled to the next bookcase. He stuck his head out . . .

And looked straight into a pair of eyes. Not Tilly Perkins's eyes. Glittering eyes! Eyes glowing in the beam of the flashlight lying on the floor. Aaaah, thought Jeff, but he didn't yell out loud. He couldn't. The sound stuck in his throat.

Chapter 11

Sir Jeff

The flashlight went out. The eyes stopped glowing.

"Got you!" yelled Tilly Perkins. "Take that. And that. Ouch!"

Jeff jumped to his feet. In the dark he bumped his head against a bookcase. It really hurt, but there was no time to rub his head. Tilly was in trouble. He grabbed the flashlight and shook it until it flickered on.

Then he saw her. She was rolling around on the floor between the bookcases. Her arms were wrapped around the worm. The worm's tail was wrapped around Tilly. They rolled around together. First Tilly was on top, then the worm. Jeff rolled his eyes.

"Help!" Tilly cried.

The others rushed in and the lights blazed on.

"What's happening?" cried Bruno. "Where's the thief?"

"Down here," Tilly panted. "The dragon's squishing me."

"Get out of that," Bruno said. He grabbed Tilly Perkins by the arm and tried to pull her away from the worm.

Tilly stayed put. Bruno grabbed both her arms and yanked. He couldn't move her.

"Tilly Perkins, get up," Jeff yelled. He was mad at Tilly for spoiling their plans. He was mad because his head hurt. "We'll never catch the real thief now," he said.

Just then a terrible racket broke out. It sounded like someone clanging a dozen saucepans together.

"The thief!" gasped Poppy Rose.

It sounded like someone thumping a big bass drum.

"A gang of thieves!" gulped Sally.

"They can't scare me," said Bruno, his eyes bulging. "Go get 'em, Jeff. I'm right behind you." He pushed Jeff from behind.

With a clang, the lid flew off the garbage can. "Eeeeeeh!" squealed Bertha. Her head popped up like a cork. "The lid jammed," she said. "I couldn't get out."

One of the tall bookcases teetered. Mr. Bronski caught it just before it crashed.

Ferdinand rolled off one of the shelves. "Wheeew!" wheezed Ferdinand. "Those shelves are a tight fit," he said. "I got stuck."

"Bertha and Ferdinand," cried Poppy Rose.

"Some thieves!" said Bruno in disgust.

Pesky kids, thought Jeff. How did they get here?

"Save me," screamed Tilly. "The dragon's got me in its clutches."

"Oh no! Our worm's squeezing Tilly," cried Bertha. She jumped around like a grasshopper.

"It's devouring her," cried Ferdinand.

"I'll save her," cried Bertha. She snatched the dragon's tail. It slipped out of her grasp. Bertha sat down with a thump.

"Death to the dragon," yelled Ferdinand. He threw himself on top of Tilly. Tilly and the worm rolled over. Ferdinand was squashed underneath.

Bruno tried again. "I can't budge her," he said. "That worm's got rocks inside it."

"What a wimp," said Poppy Rose.

"We'll make Tilly Perkins get up," said Sally. "Let the super sleuths show you how."

Poppy hooked her arms under Tilly's. Sally hung onto the worm's tail.

"Go!" cried Poppy Rose.

Poppy Rose pulled Tilly. Sally yanked the worm's tail.

"Hurry," yelled Bertha. She jumped up and down and held her nose. "Dragons have bad breath."

"Halitosis!" cried Ferdinand.

Poppy and Sally landed in a heap.

"That worm weighs a tonne," said Poppy Rose.

"It should go on a diet," said Sally.

Tilly and the worm stayed wrapped around one another.

Sally's right, thought Jeff, the worm looks really chubby.

Tilly and the worm rolled around some more.

Ferdinand squirmed out from underneath. His face was red. "Suffocating serpents!" he gasped.

"The dragon's breathing fire," yelped Tilly. "I'm hot."

Bertha burst into tears. "I can smell burning," she cried, sobbing.

"Tilly will get barbecued," cried Ferdinand. "Call the fire trucks."

Not a chance, thought Jeff. Tilly Perkins is only pretending.

Mr. Bronski stepped forward and pointed sternly at the worm. "Foul fiend! Set her free," he commanded.

The monster just grinned. Same as always, thought Jeff. But Bruno's right about the rocks. It looks really bumpy for a worm. Not at all how it used to look — smooth and sleek.

Tilly Perkins had stopped yelling. Her eyes were closed. The worm was still wrapped firmly around her.

"Somebody do something," begged Bertha.

"I'm not going near that thing," said Bruno. "I don't want to get fried."

For once, Poppy Rose and Sally had nothing to say. They looked pale.

Jeff held out his hand. "Mr. Bronski, hand me the vacuum cleaner wand, if you please. And hurry!" he said.

"Are you sure?" said Mr. Bronski.

Jeff scowled. "Yes!" he said. "I'll deal with this worm thing once and for all."

"Bravo, Jeff!" shouted Mr. Bronski. Swiftly, he brought the vacuum wand. "I dub thee Sir Jeff," he said. He tapped Jeff once on each shoulder with the vacuum wand. "Go forth, fearless knight. Fight the fearsome dragon. Good fortune go with you."

Chapter 12

Every Inch a Princess

I'll show Tilly Perkins, thought Jeff. Her and her dragons! I know who the book thief is.

Did Jeff feel pleased?

Did Jeff feel proud?

No, he did not. Jeff felt grim.

Mr. Bronski handed Jeff his shield — the garbage can lid.

"I don't need a sword or a shield," he growled. "I need a vacuum cleaner."

Mr. Bronski joined the hose to the wand. Poppy Rose and Sally plugged in the cord.

"What are you going to do?" cried Bertha.

"You can't vacuum up a humongous dragon," cried Ferdinand.

Jeff almost fell over them.

"Someone hang on to these two," he said sternly. "Keep them out of the way."

Mr. Bronski grabbed Bertha and Ferdinand. Everyone stood back. Tilly Perkins has fooled them all, thought Jeff. She's made everybody believe in the dragon. Everybody but me.

He stood alone. On each side of him the bookcases formed a narrow path. At the end of the path crouched the worm. Tilly Perkins lay wrapped in its coils.

Tilly Perkins isn't the only one who can pretend, thought Jeff. She thinks she's so smart. I'll show *her*. I'll put an end to this dragon stuff now and forever.

He held his vacuum wand before him like a knight of old. The dragon's mouth was wide open. Its throat was as red as fire. Carefully, Jeff lined up his lance. He took a deep breath.

"Dragon!" he bellowed. "Prepare to meet thy doom. Give up your treasure, or I'll run you through." The worm stayed silent. "Charge!" yelled Jeff. He plunged the wand straight down the worm's throat.

"Throw the switch," he shouted.

The vacuum roared. There was a loud sucking sound. Something banged against the end of the wand. Jeff almost lost his balance. He teetered backward.

"Lo and behold!" cried Mr. Bronski. "You have brought forth a book."

The book was too big to go down the vacuum hose. It stuck to the end.

Quick as a flash, Jeff pulled off the book. He stuck the wand down the worm's throat again. Each time Jeff poked his sword down its throat, the worm coughed up a book.

"Let me have a turn," yelled Bruno.

"Me too," yelled Poppy Rose.

"And me," added Sally.

Jeff tossed the wand to Bruno. Pretending to be a knight had been kind of fun. Now came the bad part. He had to deal with Tilly Perkins.

Tilly lay on the floor. Her magic glasses had

fallen off. Her dandelion necklace had broken.
Crushed dandelions were scattered around her.
Her eyes were closed.

"Tilly Perkins, you can get up now," Jeff said.

Bertha and Ferdinand crowded behind Jeff.
Mr. Bronski leaned over them.

"Please, Sir Jeff, make her come alive," begged Bertha, in a trembling voice.

"Tilly," Jeff said. "open your eyes. Say something."

Tilly slowly opened her eyes. "Why, it's Sir Jeff," she said.

"She's alive. She's alive," yelled Bertha.

"Sir Jeff slew the dragon," cried Ferdinand.

Jeff hauled Tilly to her feet. She staggered and looked groggy. But when she saw the books, she seemed to get stronger.

"Oh!" she cried with delight. "There's *The Dragon Hunter's Handbook*."

"And Jacobs' *English Fairy Tales*," cried Mr. Bronski. He waved it at Tilly. "My favourite."

"And *The Green Fairy Book*," yelped Bertha. "I missed it."

"And *The Red Fairy Book*," yipped Ferdinand. "I'm going to re-read it."

"Red, green, blue. There's no such thing as fairies," grumbled Bruno. "Here's *Beowulf*. It's about a monster. Now that's a good story."

"We've found the missing books," Jeff said. "I

hope you're satisfied, Tilly Perkins."

Tilly Perkins hid the books in the worm, thought Jeff. It's fun to pretend. But this time she's gone too far. Tilly Perkins is the thief.

He didn't feel mad anymore. He felt sad. He wished a dragon really had eaten the books. He wished Tilly Perkins hadn't hidden them. She should have owned up. Because of Tilly, Mr. Bronski had lost his job.

Did Tilly Perkins look regretful?

Did Tilly Perkins look repentant?

No, she did not. Tilly Perkins looked radiant. "You are a brave knight," she said. "I always knew you could slay the dragon. I'd better call my mother now. She can come and pick us up."

"She doesn't have to pick me up," said Jeff. "It's not very late. I'm going home."

"Me too," said Poppy Rose. "We've solved the case of the missing books. Right, Sally?"

Bertha fell down on her knees in front of Tilly. "We're sorry, Princess Tilly," said Bertha.

"We understood it was a bookworm,"

Ferdinand said. "Sir Jeff said so. Forgive us, Princess Tilly."

"Princess!" snorted Bruno. "Now I've heard everything."

"Stupid kids. Get up," said Poppy Rose. "You stole the books, Tilly Perkins."

"And stuffed them inside the worm," said Sally, "until you had time to take them away."

"No, she didn't," said Bertha.

"You're making a big mistake," said Ferdinand.

"Who asked you?" said Poppy Rose.

"All that stuff about the dragon was meant to throw us off the scent," said Sally. "I'm going home with Poppy Rose."

"She made us look like fools," said Bruno. "Come on, Jeff. I've got a football game to go to. No one wants to go home with you, Tilly Perkins."

Did Tilly Perkins look dismal?

Did Tilly Perkins look downcast?

No, she did not. Tilly Perkins stood tall. "Bertha and Ferdinand, you are forgiven," she said. "Promise me you'll never, ever go near a dragon again. Dragons are a bad influence. Remember that."

Tilly Perkins never gives up, thought Jeff. She shouldn't make things up. She should act like a normal person. He picked up her magic glasses. One of the arms hung loose.

"I'm afraid your glasses are broken," he said.

"You keep them, Jeff," said Tilly Perkins. "Even broken magic glasses are better than none. They help you see things more clearly."

Tilly Perkins picked up her lacy bonnet and set it on her head. She swung her shawl over her shoulders. "I believe I need fresh dandelions," she said. Then, looking every inch a princess, Tilly Perkins swept out of the library.

Tilly Perkins isn't ordinary, thought Jeff. She's remarkable. I wish I didn't have to stay mad at her.

Chapter 13

All's Well that Ends Well

Jeff wore Tilly's magic glasses at home that evening. He watched TV through them. He held his head very still to keep the broken glasses from falling off. The programmes looked the same as always. So did his family. I should have known, thought Jeff.

That night in bed he gave the glasses one more try. He stared at the ceiling through them. He thought about Tilly Perkins, and dragons, and missing books. On Monday morning he put the glasses in his pocket and took them to school.

In the playground he put on the glasses. He had to hold them on. The first thing he saw was Mr. Bronski raking the sand under the swings.

Jeff blinked.

"Mr. Bronski, you're still here!" he said.

"Forsooth! All's well that ends well," said Mr. Bronski. He had just started reading *Stories from Shakespeare*. "The principal begged my pardon. He said it was all a misunderstanding."

Jeff smiled. He turned and saw Bruno staring at the magic glasses.

"Are you crazy?" asked Bruno.

"Get lost," said Jeff.

"You don't have to tell me," said Bruno. "I don't hang around with freaks."

Poppy Rose and Sally came along. They saw Jeff wearing Tilly's glasses. Poppy Rose snickered. Sally sniggered. They dug their elbows into one another. Jeff ignored them. He waited for Tilly Perkins.

As soon as Tilly got off the school bus, Bertha and Ferdinand ran to her. Their hands were full

of dandelions. Jeff watched them through the magic glasses.

"Princess Tilly, these flowers are for you," said Bertha.

"Your Highness, may I present you with this bouquet?" asked Ferdinand.

Tilly Perkins took the flowers. "Thank you, my dears," she said. "Remember, a dragon might look harmless, but you never can tell. So *stay away from the dragon.*"

"We'll never go near it again," promised Bertha, trembling.

"On our honour," said Ferdinand, shaking.

Tilly Perkins sure knows how to scare them, thought Jeff. She's the only one who does, too. He waited for Bertha and Ferdinand to scamper away.

"Why did those two bring you flowers?" he asked Tilly.

"They know I like them," said Tilly.

"Tilly Perkins, I know who stole the books," said Jeff. "It was Bertha and Ferdinand. They were always fooling around with that worm.

They stuffed the books inside it."

"Why would Bertha and Ferdinand steal books?" asked Tilly.

"Because I was stupid," said Jeff. "I told them the dragon was a bookworm. Bookworms eat books."

"Feed their favourite books to the dragon!" said Tilly Perkins. "It doesn't make sense."

"Oh yes, it does," said Jeff. "They'd read all those books. They wanted to get rid of them. They figured Mrs. Page would buy new ones."

Did Tilly Perkins look amazed?

Did Tilly Perkins look awed?

Yes, she did.

"You knew all the time," said Jeff. "But you didn't want to tell on Bertha and Ferdinand. So you made up all that stuff about the dragon. You knew they'd believe you. They have good imaginations. You said so yourself."

"Jeff," said Tilly. "What makes you so sure?"

"The magic glasses," said Jeff. "They helped me see things clearly."

Tilly smiled at Jeff. He took off the glasses and gave them to her.

"I'm sorry I ever suspected you," he said. "I should have known better. Bertha and Ferdinand sure caused a lot of trouble."

Tilly Perkins looked solemn. "They weren't to blame, Jeff. The dragon had them in its power. I tried to tell everybody it was dangerous, but nobody believed me."

"Tilly Perkins," said Jeff, "you don't really, truly believe in dragons, do you?"

"For sure," said Tilly Perkins.

Jeff couldn't see her eyes. They were hidden under her wide-brimmed straw hat. "If dragons are evil, how come you like them so much?" he asked.

"All dragons aren't evil," said Tilly Perkins. "Some are good, I like to learn all I can about dragons. Then I know how to deal with them."

I'll never win an argument with Tilly Perkins, thought Jeff.

"And if I ever need a dragon slayer again," Tilly went on, "I'll send for Sir Jeff. He's the bravest, gentlest, truest knight in the country."

"Oh no, I'm not," said Jeff. "I'm just plain Jeff Brown." He looked thoughtful. "Still, you have to keep your imagination sharp. You never know. Even an ordinary guy like me might have to fight a dragon sometime."

Brenda Bellingham was born in Liverpool, England,
and now makes her home in Alberta. She has two
children, both grown up, and a cat named Mao, who
may or may not be grown up — he won't tell his age
to anyone.

Brenda has published three other books with
Scholastic, *The Curse of the Silver Box*, *Two Parents
Too Many* and *Princesses Don't Wear Jeans*, as well as
Joanie's Magic Boots (Tree Frog Press) and *Storm Child*
(Lorimer). She is working on several new projects
including some more stories about Tilly and Jeff.
When she is not writing, she teaches courses and
visits schools, or reads or knits.